# Jake Reynolds:

## CHICKEN OR EAGLE?

# Jake Reynolds:

## CHICKEN OR EAGLE?

SARA LEACH

ORCA BOOK PUBLISHERS

**Library and Archives Canada Cataloguing in Publication**

Leach, Sara, 1971-
Jake Reynolds : chicken or eagle? / written by Sara Leach.

ISBN 978-1-55469-145-6

I. Title.

PS8623.E253J33 2009 jC813'.6 C2009-902806-9

First published in the United States, 2009
**Library of Congress Control Number**: 2009928212

**Summary**: Jake dreams of being a superhero, but he's not exactly brave, especially when it comes to the wolves on the island where he and his family are staying.

Orca Book Publishers gratefully acknowledges the support for its publishing programs provided by the following agencies: the Government of Canada through the Book Publishing Industry Development Program and the Canada Council for the Arts, and the Province of British Columbia through the BC Arts Council and the Book Publishing Tax Credit.

Typesetting by Bruce Collins
Cover artwork by Ken Dewar
Author photo by Bob Brett

ORCA BOOK PUBLISHERS
PO Box 5626, STN. B
VICTORIA, BC CANADA
V8R 6S4

ORCA BOOK PUBLISHERS
PO Box 468
CUSTER, WA USA
98240-0468

www.orcabook.com
Printed and bound in Canada.
Printed on 100% PCW recycled paper.

12 11 10 09 • 4 3 2 1

To Ben and Julia

# Chapter One

Jake kicked at an empty crab shell. He flipped it over with the toe of his sandal, exposing the fuzzy bits that stuck out from the sides of the crab like thick whiskers. His long shadow extended over the rocky beach. Part of his brain was aware of the crab and the rocks, but part of it kept thinking about the wolf.

His best friend, Emily, fidgeted beside him. "C'mon, Jake," she said, grabbing his arm and pulling him down the beach.

He pulled away from her grasp. "I don't know, Emily. Mr. Timmins is supposed to be kind of creepy. And he doesn't like visitors."

"Don't be such a chicken," Emily said. "He can't be that bad." She put her hands on her hips. "I thought you wanted to talk to him about the wolf. The wolf you claim is on the island."

"There really is a wolf. I'm sure of it."

Emily rolled her eyes. "Uh-huh. Sure. A wolf on Hidalgo, the safest place in the world."

Jake opened his mouth to argue with her. Emily held up a hand to cut him off.

"Don't bother," she said. "I've heard it all before. That's why we have to talk to Mr. Timmins."

Jake squinted through the heat waves coming off the sand and rocks that stretched toward Mr. Timmins's house. The faded wood of the cabin blended into the forest around it, but even this far away, Jake could see the bright orange buoys hanging off the deck. Flashes of silver glinted in the afternoon sun. Jake wondered what was shining. It was like a lighthouse, warning people to stay away. He wanted to talk to the man who claimed to have seen a wolf, but he hadn't planned on marching up to his house and asking him about it.

He'd heard that Mr. Timmins once used a shotgun to scare away some older kids. He hadn't fired it, but still.

Emily flapped her arms and imitated a chicken. "*Bawk, bawk, bawk.*"

“I’m not a chicken.” Jake’s face flushed. “I’ll come. But if something bad happens, I’m blaming you.” He scuffed across the beach to the edge of the water and splashed through it, churning up the calm surface with his feet. Emily followed him. She was always looking for fun things to do and getting them into trouble. Like the time she’d convinced him to slide down the sand-banks even though they were out of bounds, and he’d jabbed his foot on a stick and had to go to the hospital on the mainland for three stitches.

“You don’t have to be mad,” she said.

Jake crossed his arms and pressed his lips together. He stared at the ocean. “I’m not.”

“Whatever.”

On the horizon, a line of white smoke twisted into the air from the pulp mill on Vancouver Island. Jake was glad the smell from the mill didn’t reach Hidalgo. It reminded him of farts—the silent ones his dad let out and pretended weren’t his.

“Hey!” Something was running down his back. It tickled, and then it pinched. He flapped his shirt and twisted around, trying to see what it was. Emily doubled over laughing. Jake hopped up and down until the pinching stopped and a small purple crab dropped into the water. It drifted to the rocks on the bottom, its pincers raised in attack mode.

Emily covered her mouth with her hands and giggled, her eyes dancing.

Jake brushed water droplets and wet sand off his neck. "Why'd you do that?"

"Relax. It was only a rock crab," Emily said. "Their pincers are smaller than my pinky nail. There's no way it hurt."

Jake thought about turning around and going home. Why should he risk getting shot by a crazy old man? But Mr. Timmins was the only one—other than Jake—who believed there was a wolf on the island. Jake was sick of Emily making fun of him for believing in the wolf. Maybe Mr. Timmins would have some proof.

A clump of feathery seaweed floated past his leg. He scooped up a handful and threw it at Emily. The bright green goo landed on her head and stuck out in clumps on her black hair. A blob of seaweed was glued to the end of her nose like a wart. She looked like a witch—a witch wearing board shorts and a bathing suit.

"Nice hair," he said. Before she could answer, he took off toward Mr. Timmins's cabin.

"I'll get you!" Emily called after him. He heard the smile in her voice. That was one good thing about Emily. She wasn't grossed out by things like seaweed or crabs.

It wasn't easy, running on the rocky beach that stretched from Emily's cabin, past his and halfway to Mr. Timmins's place. He had to pick his way, choosing the bigger rocks and staying away from slimy seaweed. He didn't want to fall and land on the sharp barnacles super-glued to nearly every surface. Emily wobbled along the rocks a few paces behind him. They were like two turtles racing.

When Jake reached the sand flats, he broke into a sprint. Emily couldn't keep up with him. He'd grown a lot during fifth grade, and this summer he was half a head taller than her, even though they were the same age.

"Stop!" she called. "I see something on that boulder."

Jake sprinted across the sand. He wasn't falling for that old trick.

"I'm not joking. I think it's a seal pup."

Jake slowed to a walk and shaded his eyes from the sun shimmering on the water. He squinted at the boulders that stuck out of the sand like domed tents scattered across a field.

Emily caught up to him and pointed to one below the tide line. "It *is* a seal pup," she whispered. "Isn't it adorable?"

With its soot gray body, pointy nose and whiskers, the seal reminded Jake of a black Lab puppy. Except it had dark almond-shaped eyes with no white around them. It stared at Jake and Emily without blinking.

Jake looked around for an adult seal, but couldn't see one. Wasn't it scared without its mom?

"It must be abandoned," he said.

"No, it isn't," Emily said. "Its mother must have left it here for the day while she went fishing. The pup is safer on the rock. The mom will be back when the tide comes up."

"How do you know?" he asked.

"I read it in a book."

Jake snorted. "That's how you know everything."

Emily frowned and scrunched up her face. She brushed the hair out of her eyes and said, "So what's wrong with reading? You read."

"Yeah, but I don't show off by repeating everything I learn."

"That's not fair." Emily kicked at the sand. "I'm only telling you so you won't hurt the seal." As she spoke, the seal pup wobbled over to the far side of the boulder.

"It's okay," Jake said to the pup as though he were talking to a baby. "We won't hurt you. Emily's just getting a little excited."

The seal flattened itself to the boulder and studied them.

Emily pulled at Jake's shirt. "We're scaring it. Let's move away. Or is saying that showing off?"

"Of course not. Anyone can figure that out." Jake followed her, tripping on rocks as he looked over his shoulder at the seal pup.

Emily stalked up the beach and sat on a log, shoulders hunched, her back to Jake.

He sat beside her. If she stayed mad, maybe she'd forget about going to see Mr. Timmins. Except he hated having her mad at him. And he really wanted to know if Mr. Timmins had seen a wolf. He wondered if the wolf would try to eat a seal pup.

"I'm sorry, okay?" Jake said. "I shouldn't have called you a show-off. But you do sound like a book sometimes." He sat beside her. "Why do you read so much? Don't you have friends and stuff at home in Vancouver?"

Emily pulled at a strand of hair. "Sure, but I don't have a TV at home. My parents don't think it's good for me. So I have lots of time to read."

Jake thought about the shows he watched during the school year. He couldn't watch them at Hidalgo because their cabin had no electricity, which meant no TV, no video games and no movies.

"Don't you wish you could watch *Megafly* or *Jungle Hunters*? They're my favorite shows."

"Huh?" Emily said.

"You know, Megafly—he's a superhero. Or Mad Torpedo. He shoots through the water, suctions himself onto boats and then climbs on board and gets the bad guys."

Emily rolled her eyes. "No, don't really miss it."

Jake shook his head. He couldn't believe she'd never even heard of them.

A bird called in the distance. *Cheeeee-cheeeee-cheee-cheee.*

Jake scanned the tops of the trees. "Look, a bald eagle."

A white-headed bird lifted off a tree and soared over their heads. Its enormous black wings stretched wide as it floated high above the beach. It glided on the air currents, turning in huge circles without seeming to move even a feather.

"Eagles chirp like robins or some other little bird," Jake said. "How can such a big animal have such a tiny voice?"

"Yeah, it's weird," Emily said.

Jake waited for her to go on, sure she'd know why eagles sounded like that, but she didn't say anything.

The eagle circled around and started to descend.

"It spotted something," Jake said.

It dropped toward the water, hitting the brakes—wings spread, talons reaching in front of its body.

Jake jumped off the log. "It's going for the seal pup. We have to rescue it!" He ran to the boulder, waving his arms in the air. "Get out of here!"

"Stop, Jake." Emily grabbed him by the shirt. He stumbled and fell on the sand.

"What are you doing? The eagle is going to get the seal pup." Jake struggled to his feet and tried to go after the eagle, but Emily grabbed his ankle, and he tumbled to the ground again.

Jake watched in horror as the eagle flew closer and closer to the seal. He cringed as the sun flashed on the hunter's sharp talons. Those things would *hurt.*

As the eagle lowered its legs and closed its talons, the seal pup wobbled to the side of the boulder and tumbled into the water with a high-pitched bark.

The eagle rose from the water and flew off, talons empty.

Jake exhaled. The eagle set down and perched on a log farther along the beach, staring at the empty rock. The pup must have swum to deeper water, because eventually the bird flew away.

Jake stood up, brushed the sand off his shorts and scowled at Emily. "Why did you tackle me?"

Emily knelt in the sand. "Are you sure you want to know, or would it be *showing off*?"

"If you don't tell me why you threw me down, I'm going to cream you," Jake huffed.

"Because that eagle was doing its job," Emily said. "He has to eat too. Just because you think the seal pup is cute doesn't mean the eagle can't eat it. If it was going for a salmon, would you have stopped it?"

Jake opened his mouth to say "of course." Then he remembered that he'd had salmon for dinner the other night. "I guess not," he mumbled.

"Then let's go to Mr. Timmins's house before you decide to play superhero again."

Jake had almost forgotten about Mr. Timmins. "I wasn't trying to be a superhero," he said.

He dusted off his hands and glanced at the cabin. It looked even more ominous now that they were closer. It glared at him like a scruffy pirate's face. Two big windows formed the eyes. Rusted chains hung on the walls like scarred cheeks. A string of football-shaped Styrofoam floats looked like the chipped teeth of a pirate who hadn't brushed for years. Orange buoys hung off the left side of the deck like an earring. Jake could hardly look at the place where the nose should be, because it reflected the afternoon sun so brightly. What was it made of? The wall between the windows seemed to be made of something metallic. White blobs were scattered across the deck. "Are those bones?" he asked.

"I think they're shells," Emily said.

"He's probably not even there," Jake said. "Why don't we go home and build a raft?"

"You're the one who wants to know if there's a wolf."

"I know there's a wolf," he said. "You just don't believe me."

"Then let's get going."

Jake sighed. What would he do when he proved there really was a wolf? He imagined what Megafly would do. He wouldn't think twice about it. He'd use his ultra-powerful laser vision to spot the wolf through the trees, wrestle it to the ground with his bare hands and then fly it off to another island, where it could hunt something other than humans.

"What are you doing?" Emily asked.

Jake's arms were out, as if he were flying over the water. He dropped them to his sides. "Nothing."

Emily smirked. "Are you coming or what, Megafly?"

Jake scratched his freckles to hide his red cheeks. "Let's go."

With each step he felt less like a superhero and more like his old, scared self. He looked at the shiny spot on the house again.

Last summer, Jake's dad had read him *Treasure Island*. Since then he'd dreamed of discovering pirate treasure. He'd also had nightmares about Captain Long John Silver. Had Mr. Timmins put a mirror on his deck to signal pirates?

# Chapter Two

Jake's feet were glued to the bottom step. Maybe Mr. Timmins was a pirate, and nobody on the island knew. Maybe he'd been waiting years for the opportunity to capture a couple of kids, tie them up in his pirate house and hold them for ransom until their parents gave him all their money.

Emily pushed past him. "Hello? Is anybody home? Mr. Timmins, are you here?"

"Stop," Jake whispered. She ignored him. He tiptoed onto the deck behind her. No one answered. He breathed a sigh of relief. Now they could go home.

He stepped closer to the cabin. The shiny area wasn't a mirror. Hundreds of pop cans had been flattened and nailed to the wall. Maybe that's why the beaches at Hidalgo were so clean. Maybe Mr. Timmins picked up everything that washed ashore and attached it to his house.

Emily pressed her hands and face up against the window. "I can't see him."

"He's not here. Let's go before he comes back and kidnaps us."

Emily lifted her head from the glass. "What are you talking about?"

"Nothing." He never should have asked his dad to read *Treasure Island* to him. It made him suspicious of everything. He'd stick to Megafly from now on.

"You've got to see this, Jake. It's amazing." Emily waved him forward.

"We shouldn't be here if he's not home."

Emily grabbed his arm and pulled him to the window. "He won't know."

Jake checked over his shoulder before he looked through the window. A mosaic of beach glass covered an entire wall. Pieces of weather-beaten glass—blue, green, brown, white, yellow—were stuck to the wood panels.

"Don't you see it?" Emily asked.

"What, the beach glass?" Jake said.

"Look harder."

Jake frowned. What was Emily talking about? She was still pressed up against the window. He shaded his eyes and looked again.

It was as though the pieces had shifted. Suddenly a severe-looking eagle glared right at him. Jake stepped away from the window. He couldn't believe someone had made such a real-looking picture out of pieces of glass.

The front door was open a crack. Emily reached for the handle.

"What are you doing?" Jake said.

"I want to see that up close. I can't believe no one's ever told me about it."

"You can't go in there!" Jake tried to pull her back. "It's called breaking and entering. You could go to jail."

"Oh, give it up." Emily pushed on the door. "You know that an open door means 'come in' on Hidalgo. If he comes home, we'll say we needed to borrow a bird book or something."

Jake twisted his hands together. Even though they weren't breaking any laws on the island by going in, he still didn't think Mr. Timmins would be too happy about it. Then again, he didn't want to stay outside alone either.

The chains clanked in the wind. Jake jumped and followed Emily through the door, leaving it open behind him.

Emily ran her fingers across the mosaic. "Imagine how many years it must have taken to collect all these pieces," she said. "Look, the wings are actually brown. I guess there isn't much black glass around."

Jake barely heard her, because his pounding pulse blocked out the sound of her voice. He turned in a slow circle, looking for Mr. Timmins. The room was much smaller than the living room at his family's cabin. The mosaic hung above a small sitting area with a worn couch and a coffee table made from an old chest with a brass lock. Maybe that was where Mr. Timmins kept the pirate's gold. Bird guides lay scattered across the chest, along with a pair of binoculars.

The kitchen sink was full of dirty dishes. Jake's mom would have had a fit if she'd seen it. Jake's family wasn't allowed to leave any dishes out, because they would attract mice and ants.

A small dining-room table filled an alcove to Jake's right. Candles and oil lamps covered most of its surface. A book of crosswords and a dictionary lay on one end.

Jake turned to the wall behind him. He gasped.

"What?" Emily said.

Jake could only point. The wall was covered in skulls. Small skulls, big skulls.

A shotgun hung in a rack above them.

"Let's get out of here." His voice came out as a squeak.

"Because he collects deer and cow skulls?" Emily asked.

Jake looked more closely at the skulls. People didn't have horns. And they didn't have long pointy jawbones either. He breathed out.

"I still think we should get out of here. Look at that shotgun."

"I'm sure he didn't kill them all."

"How can you be so sure?"

Emily shrugged. "There's no hunting allowed on Hidalgo. Anyway, there's not much more to learn without talking to him," Emily said. "Let's go."

He turned to leave, but a large figure stood in the doorway, blocking the light.

Jake stepped back onto Emily's foot. They were trapped.

The figure loomed over him. As Jake leaned back, trying to get away from him, he recognized Mr. Timmins.

"What are you doing here?" the old man asked.

Jake opened his mouth to speak, but the words froze in his throat. If they got out of here alive, he was going to kill Emily.

"We came to, uh, borrow a bird book," Emily said. "We saw this strange bird on the beach."

It sounded like a lame excuse now that she was saying it. Mr. Timmins put his hands on his hips and squinted in disbelief. Jake could see stains on his gray T-shirt and little bits of food in his white beard.

"Actually..." Jake cleared his throat. He checked behind Mr. Timmins, looking for bags of treasure or kidnapped children, but saw only trees and deck. He cleared his throat again. The words came out slowly. "We came by to see if you knew anything about the wolf. And then we saw the mosaic." He was speaking faster now. The words tumbled out of his mouth.

"It was so amazing we had to come in and look at it. How did you make it? The eagle looks so real."

Mr. Timmins relaxed his arms by his sides. His face softened. He looked over Jake's shoulder at the mosaic. "It is beautiful, isn't it? My wife made it for me many years ago. She's dead now." He paused for a moment. Then he grunted. "May I come in?"

"Sorry," Jake said. He and Emily stepped back into the house.

"Well, you've already invited yourselves in, so you might as well make yourselves comfortable."

Jake edged toward the door. He wasn't sure he could get comfortable in this house, especially with the shotgun hanging on the wall.

But Emily was already walking over to look at the books on the chest. "Mr. Timmins, is it true that you've seen a wolf on the island?"

"Now who told you that?" he asked.

"I overheard my parents talking about it," Jake said.

Mr. Timmins harrumphed. "They probably thought I made it up, didn't they?"

Jake nodded. "They said you must have seen a dog and imagined it was a wolf."

Mr. Timmins ran his fingers over the glass of the mosaic. He spoke softly. "Nobody believes me anymore. They all think I'm an old geezer who's seeing things." He spun around to face them. "Well, I'm not!" he shouted.

Jake jerked backward.

"Do you think the wolf is still on the island?" Emily asked.

Mr. Timmins crouched down and put his face close to hers. "Why do you want to know?"

"Jake thinks there is. I don't believe him," Emily said.

He looked over at Jake. "What makes you think that?"

"I saw clumps of gray hair stuck to a tree. There aren't any dogs that color around here."

Mr. Timmins nodded. "It's possible."

"I told you so," Jake said to Emily.

"You haven't proved anything yet," Emily said.

Mr. Timmins pulled a thick book off the shelf. "I saw a wolf on the old logging road that leads to Miguel Bay," he said. "It could be anywhere on the island though."

"How did you know it was a wolf?" Emily asked.

"Because he left tracks in a straight line. A dog's tracks go from side to side." He opened the book. "Here's a picture of a gray wolf. Take a look."

"How could you tell it was a gray wolf?" Emily asked.

"Good question. The gray wolf is the most common kind in British Columbia. It's possible it could be a different kind, but I doubt it."

Jake wished he'd thought to ask a good question too.

He looked at the photo. Emily's breath warmed his shoulder as she stood on her tiptoes to get a look. The wolf had a face like a dog's but bigger, with blue eyes and patches of white and gray fur. "Thanks." He started to close the book.

"Wait." Emily stuck her hand out to stop him. "I'm still reading what it says."

"You're only supposed to look at the picture, not read the whole book," Jake said.

Emily frowned. "Maybe you should try reading more. You might learn a thing or two."

"Do you two always argue like this?" Mr. Timmins asked. He gave the book to Emily. "Finish the page quickly. Then you two need to scram. It's time for my nap."

Jake studied the skulls while he waited. "Did you kill all those animals?"

Mr. Timmins grinned. "Wouldn't you like to know."

Jake gulped.

"So if there really is a wolf, how did it get to Hidalgo?" Emily asked.

Mr. Timmins pointed to a large green island visible across the channel. "Probably swam over from Mercedes," he said. "If there are too many wolves in an area, they'll force the weakest one to leave."

"That's so mean," Jake said.

Mr. Timmins shrugged. "It's the way of the world." He took the book from Emily. "Don't you two go searching out that wolf, understand?" He glared at them, one after another.

Jake nodded vigorously. Emily dipped her chin.

"Wolf attacks on humans are rare, but like any wild animal marking its territory, they're unpredictable. Unless you're on Cook's Point where there are lots of cabins and people, stay out of the forest."

Jake nodded again.

"If we run into a wolf, what should we do?" Emily asked.

Mr. Timmins frowned. "I said don't go looking for the wolf."

"We won't," she said. "But if there really was a wolf on the island, I'd want to be prepared."

He nodded. "Fair enough. If you see a wolf, never do anything to make it come closer to you."

"Well, duh," interrupted Jake. "Who would want to do that?"

"Shh," Emily said.

"If it comes close, or you think it might attack, make lots of noise, throw things at it and back away." Mr. Timmins pointed a finger in Jake's face. "NEVER run."

Jake tried not to flinch, to stand still like he would if a wolf were about to attack him, but his hands flew to his chest.

Mr. Timmins grinned and shooed them out the door. "Next time you come to see me, I'll have a surprise for you."

"What is it?" Emily asked.

"I'll tell you next time you come. Now let an old man get some rest."

# Chapter Three

Jake woke in the middle of the night with his heart pounding. Something had startled him out of a dream. What was it?

He strained his eyes to see in the dark. A beam of moonlight shone through the skylight, allowing him to see the outline of the other bunk bed. His younger sister Sierra's breathing was the only sound in the bunkhouse. Had he heard his parents moving around in the main cabin? He didn't think so.

Then he heard the noise again. Howling.

*Aaaaroooh-rooooh.*

Jake pulled the covers up to his chin. It was the loneliest sound he had ever heard. The hair on his arms and legs prickled against the sheets. Maybe it was Scout, the Campbells' dog. Except Scout had never howled like that before.

*Roooh-ooh-rooooh-ooh*. The howl went up and down like an ambulance's siren, then petered out before starting again. Jake pulled the covers over his head, but he could still hear it.

The howling continued for another minute, and then it stopped. Jake lay silent, listening. He imagined a wolf creeping around the bunkhouse, sniffing the air, waiting for its chance to attack the two kids inside.

"Stop it," he whispered to himself, trying to push aside the thought. He listened. No more howls. For all he knew, the wolf could have been on the other side of the island. On a calm night, sounds traveled across the ocean so clearly they could sometimes hear music coming from the cabins on Mercedes Island.

He tried to go back to sleep, but his heart was pounding too loudly. Every noise made him jump. Branches scratched the window. Sierra snorted in her sleep.

In his mind, the wolf crept closer.

Jake tried to banish the image. He imagined throwing a net over the wolf, wrapping it up tightly and dragging it out of his mind. It worked for a while, and he was able to relax a bit, but the wolf kept escaping from the net and creeping up on him again.

"But I don't want to take her to George's," Jake said to his mom. His eyes felt heavy and scratchy from his being awake the night before. He must have fallen asleep eventually, but it felt like he'd been awake for hours.

His mom cracked an egg so hard that half the shell fell into the mixing bowl. "I want to get this baking finished, and then I'm going to clean the cabin. If you'd prefer, I can take Sierra, and you can wash the floor."

Sierra skipped into the cabin from the back deck. "Let's go, Jakey," she called. "I wanna see the chickens."

Jake sighed. Sierra was already slipping her feet into her sandals. If his dad was here, he could take her on the walk. If his dad was here, his mom wouldn't need a break in the first place.

"She'll never make it all the way," Jake said. George's house was halfway to the other end of the island.

It took Jake over an hour to walk there. How long would it take a three-year-old?

"She's done it before," his mom said. "Emily's coming, right? I'm sure the two of you can carry her for a while if she gets tired."

"What if we see the wolf?" Jake asked.

"How many times do I have to tell you? There's no wolf on the island. It's a rumor."

"But last night I heard howling."

"That was a dog," his mom said.

Sierra grabbed their mom's leg. "Mommy, will the big bad wolf eat me up?"

Jake's mom threw him a look as if to say, *See what you've done?* She knelt in front of Sierra and gave her a hug. "There's no wolf and nothing to worry about. Have a good time with your big brother."

"And Emily!" Sierra ran out the door. Emily was waiting in the driveway. Her black ponytail flew in the air as she jumped off a stump and landed in the dirt, creating a cloud of dust. Sierra climbed up on the stump and jumped into Emily's arms.

Jake's mom handed him a backpack. "There are lots of treats in here. You can use them to bribe her up the hill."

"Is there anything for me?"

"Of course, but leave enough for Sierra. You can get George to give you a ride home in the truck. Have fun." She ushered him out the door. Jake had the feeling she couldn't wait for them to leave.

He ran down the dirt road and caught up with Emily and Sierra.

"Thanks for coming," he said to Emily. "I can't believe my mom is making us do this, especially with a wolf out there."

"We'll be on the main road. Not in the forest."

Sierra took three times as long to walk the same distance as Jake. It wasn't just that her legs were shorter. She stopped to inspect pinecones, shuffle her feet in the dirt and pick salal berries, even if they weren't ripe.

"This is going to take forever," Jake groaned.

"So what?" Emily said. "We've got all day."

Sierra ran over and grabbed Emily's hand. "Want a salal berry?"

"Thanks." Emily popped the purple berry into her mouth and grimaced. "Sierra, these are so sour, how can you eat them?"

"They're yummy," Sierra said.

"Don't I get one?" Jake asked.

Sierra shook her head. "Only Emily."

Jake frowned. He knew he shouldn't care that Sierra hadn't given him a sour berry, but it bothered him that she liked Emily so much. Why did she think Emily was so perfect? She was just a girl who read a lot of books. She wasn't that special.

Jake heard something rustling in the bushes. He stepped back. His heart pounded. Was that the wolf? A black shape jumped out and ran at him.

"Aaagh!" He threw his arms in front of his face.

"It's just Scout," Emily said. "Don't be scared." She let the black Lab sniff her hand, and then she rubbed his head.

Jake relaxed. "I wasn't scared. He surprised me, that's all."

Emily raised her eyebrows.

"He was running straight at me."

"But it wasn't something scary. It was this sweet, adorable dog." She made kissing noises in Scout's ear. "Besides, what could hurt you on the island?"

"You mean other than a wolf?" Jake said.

"There aren't any wolves on Cook's Point. Mr. Timmins already said that."

"Did you hear something last night?" Jake asked.

Emily tilted her head and gave him a questioning look. Obviously she hadn't heard anything. Maybe he'd imagined the whole thing.

Sierra's eyes were as big as sand dollars as she looked back and forth between Emily and Jake, listening to every word.

"What if the wolf tries to eat us?" she said.

"It won't. But even if it did, I'd protect you," Jake said.

"Right. By running away when it jumps at her?" Emily laughed.

Jake scowled. "That's not fair!"

Emily held Sierra's hand. "There's nothing dangerous on Hidalgo."

Jake took Sierra's other hand in his. "Except for the red jellyfish and the oysters," he said.

Sierra nodded. "Jake cried when the jellyfish stung him. They're bad."

Jake blushed at the thought of crying in front of everybody at the beach. Megafly wouldn't have cried. But the jellyfish sting had hurt so much he'd thought his leg was going to fall off.

Emily stroked Scout's black coat. "The jellyfish are in the water, not on the island, and since when is an oyster a dangerous animal?"

"An oyster cut Jakey's foot once," Sierra said. "He had to soak it in a bowl of hot water with stinging stuff that Mommy poured in."

"If you can't be bothered to wear shoes on the beach, of course you're going to get cut," Emily said.

"You don't always wear shoes on the beach," Jake said.

"I do when we're on a beach full of rocks and oysters."

They reached the bottom of the big hill that separated Cook's Point from the rest of the island.

"I'm tired," Sierra said.

"We haven't even started up the hill," Jake said.

Sierra plunked down in the dirt.

"Please, Sierra, let's get going. Look, Scout's already halfway up."

Sierra shook her head.

"I thought you wanted to see the chickens."

"Carry me."

Jake shook his head. "We'll never get you all the way up the hill."

Emily walked a few paces ahead of them. "Hey, Sierra, look at all the salal berries up here."

Sierra jumped up and ran to the salal bush. The small berries hung at her eye level amidst the thick green leaves. She picked a handful and had just started to sit down when she pointed to something on the ground.

"Dog poo!" she said.

Emily leaned closer to it.

"Ew!" Sierra said. "Don't touch it!"

"I'm just looking at it," Emily said. "It doesn't look like dog poo. See, it has lots of hair in it."

"Uh-oh," Jake said.

"What?" Emily asked.

"*W-o-l-f.*"

Emily waved her hand, like she was brushing away the idea. "It is not."

Sierra planted herself between them. "What are you talking about? What? Tell me!"

Jake took a deep breath. How would he get them out of this one? Suddenly he remembered the treats. He rummaged through the backpack. "*W-o-l-f* spells gummies." He held up a bag of gummy bears. "We can share them and have a long rest at the top of the hill."

He swore he could see his little sister start to drool.

"I want one now!" she yelled, lunging for the bag.

Jake stuffed them back in the pack and ran up the hill ahead of her. "You'll have to catch me first!"

Sierra ran after him, chased by Emily. "Wait up, Jakey!"

"Yeah, Jakey, wait for us!"

Jake ran to the top at a slow jog, going fast enough to keep away from Sierra, but not so fast that he was out of sight. Scout padded up and down the hill, as if to encourage her. They reached the top and collapsed on the moss by the side of the road. He dug out the bag of gummy bears and handed them to Sierra.

"Save some for us."

Scout loped along the road. Jake noticed his foot-prints in the dust. They went from side to side, like Mr. Timmins had said.

"Hey, Scout," Emily called, "you need to go home."

The dog circled back and licked Emily's legs.

She giggled. "That tickles. Now go home." She pointed down the hill.

Scout nuzzled Jake and Sierra, and then he padded off toward Cook's Point.

Jake reached for the pack of gummy bears. "Hey, there are hardly any left in here."

Sierra grinned at him. Her cheeks puffed out like two balloons. Glossy gummy bear chunks stuck to her teeth. She clutched the bag to her chest.

"Come on. Share with us."

Sierra hid the bag behind her back. "No, they're mine."

Emily laughed. "Sierra, why don't you give us each one?"

Sierra glowered at Emily, which made her laugh even harder.

Jake snorted. Emily thought it was funny because she didn't have to deal with it every day. She would feel differently if she were stuck looking after a younger sister all the time.

Emily pointed to a salal bush behind them. "Look at this spiderweb."

As Jake knelt to look, something gray flashed by in the trees. He peered into the woods, but saw nothing. "Did you see that?"

"What?" Emily said.

“Something gray in the trees.”

“Give it up,” Emily said.

“There could still be a *w-o-l-f* here,” Jake said.

Emily rolled her eyes. “Even if there was one on the island, it wouldn’t come this close during the day when there are people around.”

Jake’s shoulders drooped. Emily was right. He was reading too much into things. A lot of people walked through this area every day. Why would the wolf come near them? But he was sure he’d seen something. What would he do if the wolf attacked? His dad had told him to look after Sierra. How would he protect her?

# Chapter Four

His sister leaned across his lap to look at the web stretched between two branches of salal. Drops of moisture from the previous night's rainfall clung to its strands, making it visible next to the leaves. A black spider the size of Jake's thumbnail hung in the middle.

"It's an orb weaver," said Emily. "That's what all the spiders that build round webs are called. They usually build a new one every night. See how the spider's dropping to the ground? They do that when they're scared."

"Right," said Jake. "I knew that."

Sierra's mouth was so full of gummies she couldn't speak. She reached out a hand to touch the web. Jake grabbed her arm.

"It might bite you," he said.

Sierra snatched her arm back and swallowed. "Will I die if it bites me?" She looked ready to cry.

"No. It's not poisonous," Emily said. "And it won't bite you." She wrinkled her nose at Jake.

He threw his arms in the air. "I didn't know that. And she might have broken the web."

"The spider would build it again."

Jake sighed and turned away. There was no point trying to win an argument with Emily. The hot dusty road stretched ahead of them. This always felt like the longest part of the walk. Not a single gust of wind made it past the fir and pine trees that grew between the road and the shore. Jake guessed it would take him about half an hour to walk to the water from where they stood, but he couldn't see even a glimpse of the ocean.

He imagined the rest of the walk—past the dusty hot section, down into the bigger trees, to the top of the curving road that led down the hill to the house of the island caretaker, George. On Cook's Point, where he and Emily stayed, the cabins were pretty close together. Once they went up the big hill, though, there was nothing but road and forest through the middle of the island until they reached George's.

If he wanted to walk farther—not that he did—it would be another hour at least to the other end of the island, where more cabins were lined up along the shore. His dad had walked around the shore of the island once, and it took him almost the whole day.

Sierra crawled into his lap. "Carry me."

It was going to be a long walk.

"I see George's house!" Sierra called.

They had reached the top of the final hill. Jake breathed a sigh of relief. His arms ached from carrying Sierra. She had been okay on the downhill parts, but on the flats she had insisted that he and Emily make a chair with their hands and carry her like a princess. He didn't know how someone so small could weigh so much.

"There are the chickens," Emily said.

As they rounded the corner, the caretaker's yard came into view, nestled at the end of a deep bay. George's place looked more like a real house than any other cabin on Hidalgo. It was a two-story red building with a satellite dish and a generator that created electricity all day and night. George had electric lights and a television, as well as the only vehicle on the island.

"George is so lucky," Jake said.

"Yeah," said Emily, "he gets to stay on Hidalgo all year, not just in the summer."

"Or for only a few weeks, like me." Last year Jake's family had been able to come for the whole summer, before his dad was promoted and his mom started working again.

A series of work sheds lined the edge of the forest. Jake could see boats, generators and propane tanks sticking out of open doors.

"I guess he works pretty hard though, doesn't he?" Jake said.

"He told me once that in the summer he works from first light until dark, taking propane to the cabins and making sure everything on the island works."

Jake gazed at the huge garden, the plum trees and the chicken yard next to the house. Even with all the work, he'd still love to live there year-round. At Hidalgo, away from his school friends and his regular life, he really believed he could be a superhero, even if he never managed to do anything heroic.

Sierra ran down the hill. "Hurry up!"

"Careful on the rocks," Jake called. "They can be really—"

Sierra's foot rolled on a rock. Her momentum carried her forward, and she tumbled to the ground, landing on her chest with her arms spread in front of her.

"—slippery." He ran to catch up to her as she started to wail.

Emily sprinted for Sierra too, two steps in front of Jake. He tried to push past her, but she blocked his way and reached his little sister first.

Jake caught up and knelt beside Emily. He tried to nudge her out of the way as they brushed off his sister.

"I want Mommy!" Big tears dripped down her face and mixed with the dirt, making muddy streaks on her cheeks.

"How about a hug?" Jake asked.

Sierra shook her head and continued crying.

"I have some crackers," he said. "Will those help?"

Sierra ignored him.

Emily stroked her hair. "That must have hurt. Do you want to hold my hand the rest of the way?"

Sierra nodded, slipped her hand inside Emily's and started skipping down the hill.

Jake followed a few steps behind, scowling. He kicked a rock into the bushes. He remembered sitting on his bed with his dad the day before they left for Hidalgo.

"I don't understand why you can't come with us," Jake had said. "You've always been able to get time off before."

His dad sighed. "I've told you already. I have a conference at the end of this week. It's a big deal for my company. If I do a good job on the presentation, it will mean a lot more sales for us, and then maybe I won't have to work so hard next year. By the time I get back, you'll be only a few days from coming home, so there's no point in me going all the way up to the island."

Jake glowered. "We won't be able to go to Chipmunk Cove. And who am I going to build a fort with?"

"Your mom can drive the boat as well as I can," his dad said. "And you and Emily can build a fort without me. I'm not happy about missing out on those things either. I'll be stuck in the office while you get to play." He rumpled Jake's hair. "I need you to do something for me."

"What?" Jake didn't feel like doing anything for his dad right then. He was too grumpy.

His dad gently touched Jake's face and turned it until he was looking right at him. "Take care of Sierra. Your mom's going to need some help with her."

Jake opened his mouth to protest. Then he saw something in his dad's eyes. Maybe he really was sad about not being able to come. Jake nodded. "Okay."

His dad smiled. "That's my boy. You're her big brother. You look after her." He had kissed Jake on the head and walked out of the room.

Now Jake couldn't even make Sierra feel better when she fell. Maybe Emily should come sleep at his house, and he could go be an only child at her house. What was the point in being a big brother if Sierra wanted to spend all her time with Emily?

They made it to the bottom of the hill without any more falls. The pier stretched out before them across the muddy beach. It was low tide, and Jake could see hundreds of half-buried black sand dollars.

George strolled out of his front yard, gripping a bucket. His rough hands were covered in oil stains. He nodded to the three children and motioned toward the chicken coop with his head.

"Coming to feed the chickens?"

"Uh-huh," Jake said as they ran over to the coop. Even though he hadn't wanted to admit it to his mom, this was still one of his favorite outings on Hidalgo.

Emily pulled Sierra away from the entrance to the coop as George opened the door and twenty chickens came barreling out, squawking and flapping.

The chickens ran across the field toward the stream near the house. Jake doubled over with laughter as they bobbed and flapped and jumped into the air. He never knew what it was they were running from.

Sierra chased them. "Here chicken, here chicken," she called, making them run away even faster.

Finally they calmed down and started pecking at the ground. George sprinkled corn and seeds near them. That started another frenzy of jostling and pecking.

"Want to feed them?" he asked. "I need to pick some peas for dinner."

"Sure," Jake said. He and Emily each took a handful of feed and tossed it in front of the chickens.

"I wanna feed them too," Sierra said. She ran to George and scooped a handful of feed out of the bucket.

Instead of throwing it on the ground, though, she shoved her hand in the face of a nearby chicken.

"Watch out, Sierra," Jake said. "They might not like that." He grabbed another handful from the bucket. Within seconds a group of chickens surrounded him, stepping on his toes in their rush to get the food.

Sierra shrieked behind him. "Jaa-aaake! Help!"

Jake spun around and saw Sierra sucking on her finger. A chicken was flapping its wings in front of her. Jake tried to get to her, but he couldn't get through the circle of chickens. In his frustration he swatted at them. "Get out of here!" he shouted. Sierra flinched at his loud voice.

Emily reached her first. "Did that chicken bite you?"

Sierra nodded. Tears streamed down her face. "That's a bad chicken. They should put it in jail!" Her voice got louder with every word.

Jake smiled.

"Stop laughing at me." Her crying grew even louder.

Jake finally made it to her side. "I'm not laughing at you. I'm happy you're okay." He tried putting his arms around her, but she squirmed away from him and over to Emily.

"I'm NOT okay." She held up her finger. Suddenly the tears stopped, and she smiled. "But it's all right. Look. The chicken didn't bite off my whole finger."

Jake worked hard not to smile again. He could see a little red spot where the chicken had nipped her.

"Something wrong?" George had returned from the garden with an empty bucket.

"A chicken bit Sierra," Jake said.

Sierra held up her finger again. "But he didn't eat all of it."

George nodded. "Glad to hear it."

"Weren't the peas ready?" Emily asked.

George jerked his head toward the garden and mumbled something Jake couldn't quite hear; then he walked up to the work sheds.

"What did he say?" Sierra asked.

"I think he said to go look in the garden," Emily said.

Jake shook his head. "He said *not* to go in the garden."

Sierra ran around the corner. "I want to see the garden. Let's pick some raspberries."

Jake ran after her. Why wouldn't George want them to come around to the garden? They always went in there.

Sierra had stopped at the garden gate. "Ooh. What's that?"

Jake covered his mouth with his hand. A mess of bloody feathers and bones lay on the grass. "Uh, I think that was a chicken." He tried to grab his sister and move her away. She pulled out of his arms and bent closer.

"Is it the chicken who bit me?" Sierra asked.

Jake pulled her back. "Don't touch it."

Emily came up behind him. "Yuck."

"I told you he didn't want us to come here. Nice job. Now Sierra's seen it."

George came back with another bucket and a pair of work gloves. "That's the third chicken we've lost this week." He scooped up the pieces and threw them in the bucket. Jake pinched his nose as a warm rotten smell filled his nostrils.

"What do you think killed it?" Emily asked.

George wiped the sweat off his face. "Maybe an eagle."

Jake glanced at Emily. Maybe an eagle. Or maybe a wolf.

# Chapter Five

Jake's dad called during dinner that night. His mom excused herself from the table and took the cell phone to her bedroom. Jake ate his chicken without tasting it, wondering what they were talking about.

A few moments later she came back into the main cabin and handed Jake the phone. "Dad wants to talk to you."

He nodded. "Hi."

"Mom told me about the chickens today."

"Yeah. We walked all the way there."

"How did it go?" his dad asked.

Jake took a deep breath. "Not so well. Sometimes Sierra's hard to look after."

His dad laughed. "Yeah, I know. Mom told me about the cut finger and the scraped knees, and that she's talking about seeing chicken guts. Do you think she'll have nightmares tonight?"

Jake slumped into the chair. "I don't know. I'm not a very good big brother."

"Did you try your hardest?"

"I guess so."

"That's all anyone can do. Keep trying, okay?"

"Yeah."

"I miss you."

"Me too." Jake handed the phone back to his mom. What if trying his hardest still wasn't good enough? He shook his head and took his plate to the kitchen. He wasn't hungry anymore.

The next day Jake's mom passed him a folded slip of paper. "Mr. Timmins must have brought this by while you were at George's yesterday. I didn't notice it until this morning." She tilted her head to the side. "Since when did you become friends?"

Jake shrugged and grabbed the note. "We met him the other day. He isn't really a friend. I didn't think he liked us very much."

He opened the note.

*Jake and Emily,*

*Saw our friend. Have photos. Come by to see them. You haven't seen the surprise yet either.*

*R. Timmins*

Jake folded the note and put it in his pocket. "See you later."

"Where are you going?"

"To Emily's."

"Be back by lunchtime. I need you to look after Sierra again this afternoon."

Jake flopped back in his chair. "Not again!"

"Again."

"But I wanted to work on my comic book."

"It'll have to wait," his mom said. "You can do it later tonight."

"But it's too dark at night. The candles don't give off enough light for me to draw."

His mom narrowed her eyes. Jake knew that look. There was no point in arguing.

"Fine," he said. "I'm trying to practice my drawing like Dad said I should. I guess you don't want me to grow up to be a famous artist." He grabbed his shoes and ran out the door.

Jake leaped up the stairs to Emily's cabin and rapped on the door. When she opened it, he thrust the note into her hands. "Looks like I'm right. There is a wolf on the island."

Emily scanned the note. "We'll see." She pulled her hair into a ponytail, wrapped a bandanna around it and ran toward the beach.

Jake hurried to catch up with her as she strode along the sand to Mr. Timmins's cabin. "You're in a big rush," he said.

Emily shrugged. "I'm curious. Aren't you?"

"Yeah. But what if the wolf is still out there?"

Emily stopped and grinned at him. "Are you scared, Megafly?"

"No." But even as he said it, his heart fluttered. Of course he was scared. Who wanted to run into a wolf?

Emily set off again. "If there is a wolf, he probably saw it at night. It wouldn't be hanging out on the beach in the middle of the day."

"So now you're an expert on wolves, are you?"

"I read it in that book at Mr. Timmins's house. Maybe if you'd looked at more than the picture, you'd have learned a few things too." She pointed to the water's edge. "The geoduck spot is bare."

Jake nodded. The tide was still low. Past all the rocks stretched a smooth sandy patch that was almost always covered by the ocean. Hundreds of huge clams hid below the sand, even though the only things that showed were the tips of their long necks. He'd never found out why they were called "gooey ducks" (even though their name wasn't spelled that way). "Let's go get them!"

He held his arms out in the wind and tilted them from side to side, swerving across the beach like an airplane.

"Here's one," Emily called.

Jake flew to the right and brought his plane down for a landing in front of a brown seaweed-covered lump.

He nudged it with his toe. A stream of water squirted into the air as high as his knee.

"Nice," Emily said. She stomped beside another lump. Water shot out almost to her waist.

Once Jake and his dad had dug up a geoduck. While his dad grabbed the rubbery neck, Jake had dug around it as fast as he could with a shovel. The hole was up to his waist before they finally caught the clam. Its shell was white and slimy and as big as Jake's foot. Its neck was as long as his arm. His dad had told him that the clams shot the water into the air as they pulled their necks into the sand to hide from whatever was shaking the beach.

Jake ran up behind Emily and touched the neck of a clam. As the neck disappeared, the water squirted up the leg of her shorts.

"Aah!" She yelped and jumped away.

He grinned. "Gotcha!"

She leaped to the side and landed beside him. A geoduck squirted between them, almost as high as their chins, spraying both of their chests.

"Ugh, you got us both that time," Jake said.

"That was one of the highest squirts ever." She started running across a patch of eelgrass that lay flat and drying at low tide. Brown geoduck necks stuck through the grass every few steps. "Watch this!"

Jake laughed. It looked like Emily was playing in a fountain at a water park. With every step, plumes of water shot up around her. In her wake she left small round puddles where the necks had once been.

"Let me try," he yelled. He could only see the squirts out of the corner of his eye as he ran. The beach crackled and slopped as crabs scurried for cover and clams shot water into the air.

He reached Emily at the sand flats. They both collapsed onto the beach, panting and laughing.

Emily rolled over onto her stomach. "There's Mr. Timmins's house. Let's go."

Jake's body tensed. He felt it crackle like one of the crabs. He'd been having so much fun he'd forgotten to check for wolves. Taking a deep breath, he said, "I guess so."

They ran across the sand and up the stairs to the cabin. Mr. Timmins was waiting for them on the deck.

"So you decided to come back," he said. "Look, I have proof." He ushered them into the house and tapped a key on a computer set up on the kitchen table.

"You have a laptop?" Jake blurted.

Mr. Timmins grinned. "Solar panels and satellites are wonderful things. Now I can download the *New York Times* crossword every day." He patted Jake's back. "You believed all along. Well, here's the proof for the ones who didn't believe."

Jake felt his body grow taller. He stepped closer to the laptop to get a better view.

Mr. Timmins scrolled through some photos and clicked a button. A picture of the beach in front of his cabin enlarged on the screen.

A blurry gray streak filled one corner.

"Is that it?" Jake tried not to sound disappointed.

Mr. Timmins nodded. "That's them."

"What do you mean, them?" Emily asked.

"The wolf has a friend. A mate, I think. They were playing on the beach." He pointed to another streak. "See, they were chasing each other."

Jake's jaw dropped. "Right out here on the beach, in plain sight?" He glared at Emily. "In the middle of the day?"

"It was early in the morning," Mr. Timmins said. "I doubt that anyone else saw them. I was up bird-watching."

Emily waggled her head at Jake. "So not in the middle of the day then."

Mr. Timmins frowned at them. "Enough bickering. Wolves rarely come near people. It was a special treat for me to see them."

"It's great that you have proof," Jake said. "Now everybody will believe us. I mean you."

Mr. Timmins shut the laptop. "It's not good news. Before long someone else is bound to see them, and they'll probably want to kill them."

"No!" Emily gasped.

Jake bit his lip. He didn't want the wolves killed, but he didn't want them on their island either. If they were already attacking chickens, wouldn't they soon start attacking dogs or kids?

Mr. Timmins shook his head. "It's terrible, I know. Before long they'll be calling a special meeting, and everyone will be up in arms, telling us that the wolves should be shot." He put his hands on his hips. "Well, I won't have it!" He was almost shouting.

Jake jumped back. "What are you going to do?"

Mr. Timmins pulled at his beard. "I'm still working on a plan. But don't go telling anyone about these photos. Do you hear me?" He pushed his face right up to Jake's.

Jake took another step back and nodded. It wasn't like you could see anything in the pictures. He didn't know why Mr. Timmins was so worried.

Mr. Timmins walked to the hallway and tapped his barometer. "Storm coming soon," he said. "Not that I need this thing to tell me. I can feel it in my knees." He waved toward the door. "You two scat. I need to work on my plan."

"What about the surprise?" Emily asked.

Mr. Timmins looked startled, as though he'd already forgotten they were there. "The surprise? Oh, yes. Go around the back to the Douglas fir tree."

Jake and Emily ran down the stairs.

"I can't believe Mr. Timmins has photos. You were right all along," Emily said.

Jake grinned and clamped his mouth shut so he wouldn't say "I told you so." Then he frowned. "How come you believed two fuzzy pictures and not me?"

"Because he wouldn't have made that up," she said. "But we do need to find more evidence. Not everyone will believe those pictures."

Jake nodded, even though a part of him wished he could say Mr. Timmins was crazy, like so many people on the island did. Then he wouldn't have to believe that there were *two* wolves on the island.

Emily ran to a huge tree up the hill behind Mr. Timmins's cabin. "That must be the Douglas fir tree he's talking about."

"How do you know it's a Douglas fir?" Jake asked.

"Because my tree book says they have cork-like bark, and that the needles are about two centimeters long." She picked up a cone. "And the cones look like little mice are trying to get inside them."

Even though he was irritated by Emily spouting off again, Jake couldn't help examining the cone. "What are you talking about? I don't see any mice."

"Look carefully," Emily said. "See those flaps sticking out of each layer of the cone? Don't they look like mouse bums?"

Jake looked again. "I get it. Those thin parts are the tails."

She smiled. "Yup."

He rubbed a hand across the tree's trunk. His fingers flopped in and out of the deep ridges of the bark. "So what do you think the big deal is about the tree?"

Before Emily could answer, a huge ruckus started above them. Jake leaped away from the tree, expecting an enormous wild creature to lunge at him.

# Chapter Six

The noise sorted itself into sounds Jake could recognize—like several eagles screeching at once, only higher-pitched.

"What's that?"

"I bet there's an aerie up there," Emily said. "An eagle's nest." She started jumping up and down and pointing. "It *is* an aerie. I see one. I see an eaglet!"

"Where?"

"On the third big branch up. It doesn't have a white head. They must turn white as they get older."

Jake realized the brown lump he'd been looking at was actually a bird. He saw two more near it. "There are three of them. And look, there's the mom."

An adult eagle rested on a branch nearby, staring at Jake and Emily.

"Do you think they always make so much noise?" Emily asked.

"Maybe they're hungry." Jake pointed to the water. "Look, here comes lunch."

Another bald eagle swooped into the tree, holding a silver fish in its talons. Jake guessed it must be the father. It dropped the salmon into the nest, where it was quickly ripped apart by the smaller birds. They were quiet for a moment, and then the screeching started up again. The mother eagle took off immediately.

"It only took them a few seconds to eat that huge fish," Emily said.

"I know."

"Let's see what the mother comes back with," Jake said.

"Sure, let's wait a few minutes," Emily said.

Jake sat down on a soft patch of leaves and moss and leaned against a log. "So do you think it was the wolf that ate the chickens?"

"Probably. I know George said it was an eagle, but they hunt during the day. Don't you think someone would have seen or heard it scooping up a chicken?"

Jake smiled to himself. He loved being right. "Why didn't they hear the wolf then?"

"I bet the wolf snuck into the coop at night, killed a chicken and ate it over by the garden."

Jake shuddered. "I heard a wolf howling the other night. Maybe it was hunting the chickens."

"What? Why didn't you tell me?"

"I tried, when we were with Sierra. You didn't want to listen to anything about wolves."

"What did it sound like?"

"Scary."

Emily sat back against the log. "I wish I'd heard it too."

"Are you crazy?"

"It's not like people hear wolves howl every day," Emily said. "That's really special."

He bit his lip to hide a smile. It felt good to know something Emily didn't, even if it hadn't felt special to him at the time.

"I don't think it was howling when it attacked the chickens though," she said.

"Why not?"

"They don't howl when they're hunting, because that lets their prey know they're coming."

“That makes sense.” Jake thought about Mr. Timmins’s fuzzy pictures. “Maybe it was howling to find a mate.”

Emily nodded. “Good thinking. I guess it worked.”

Something loud cracked behind them. With his heart pounding, Jake leapt up and spun around, expecting to see fierce jaws lunging toward him.

“Oh, look,” murmured Emily. “It’s a deer with a fawn. The baby still has its white spots. Aren’t they cute?”

Jake started breathing again.

“You’re like the kid in the fairy tale who always cries wolf,” Emily whispered.

“It could have been one,” Jake said.

Emily ignored him. She was fixated on the two deer that stood frozen, their ears up and pointed toward them.

“They think we can’t see them if they don’t move,” Emily whispered.

“Well, we might not have if they’d stayed like that all along. The crashing gave them away,” Jake said.

After a few minutes, the deer relaxed and began eating the yellow heads off the hawkweed growing nearby. Jake and Emily crouched by the log.

The deer grazed their way up the hillside.

"Let's follow them," Emily said.

Jake bit his fingernail. "I don't know. They'll probably run away. Shouldn't we stay down by the beach? Mr. Timmins said not to go into the woods. Remember, the wolves were here in the morning."

"Come on, Jake, have some fun. We'll only go a little way. We can look for evidence of the wolves as we go." She tugged on his arm.

Jake paused. "Fine. But we shouldn't go too far. We're past the end of Cook's Point."

"We won't," said Emily. "Anyway, this is still part of the point. If we go up here, we come to the end of the Burtons' road, and I'm pretty sure that isn't at the top of the hill."

They followed the deer, trying not to step on any twigs. The animals didn't seem bothered by them, but to be sure, they kept back and didn't talk. The deer continued up the slope. Jake and Emily tiptoed along an overgrown path several meters away that led in the same direction. As he walked, Jake scanned the forest, making sure nothing gray and furry was watching them.

"Relax," Emily whispered. "The deer would be spooked if a wolf was following us."

Jake let out his breath. Of course he didn't need to worry. He wished he'd thought of that himself.

As they crested the slope, they saw the road to the Burtons' house. The deer crossed the road and walked into the woods on the other side. Emily raised her shoulders as if to ask, *Should we follow?*

Jake shook his head. Emily smiled and flapped her arms like wings.

"I'm not a chicken," Jake whispered. "What about the wolves?"

Emily pointed to the deer. They were completely relaxed, their heads and ears down, eating more flowers. "No wolves!"

Jake threw his hands in the air. "Fine."

They took several steps off the road toward the deer. Then Emily stepped on a rotten log. It collapsed under her foot, and she slipped to the other side.

"Ow!"

Jake ran to her side. "Are you okay?"

"It's just a scratch, but I scared the deer."

The deer had bolted at the noise. Jake watched them bound into the forest, all four legs leaving the ground. There was no point in following them now. Even if they could find them, the deer would be skittish.

"They'll come back later," Jake said.

He and Emily looked into the woods in the direction the deer had gone. A swampy clearing full of reeds lay between them and another stand of trees into which the deer had disappeared. Jake peered at something on the edge of the clearing.

"Do you see that gray thing?" he asked.

"What?"

"I think there's a tent over there. No one's allowed to camp on the island."

"So? What's the big deal?"

"The big deal is that they're breaking the rules. Maybe they're robbers who want to break into someone's cabin."

Emily smirked. "And you're going to stop them?"

This was his chance. He could be like Megafly and save the day. He'd find out who was trespassing on the island and chase them away. No one could call him a chicken anymore. "Yes." He ran around the edge of the swamp. "Let's go see what's going on."

"Leave them alone," Emily said. "They're probably just kayakers who don't know the rules. We can tell our parents when we get home."

Jake paused. Maybe they were kayakers. Or maybe they were thieves, and he'd prevent a crime if he confronted them. What would he do if someone dangerous was in that tent? He and Emily could outrun them and find someone to help, he decided.

He started pushing through the bushes again. Salal leaves and twigs scratched his face.

Emily scurried to keep up with him. "I don't think this is a good idea, Jake."

He ignored her as he followed a path around the side of the clearing. This must be where the ground was the driest, but why would anyone want to camp in the swamp?

At last he reached what he had thought was a tent. Except it wasn't one at all. It was a large gray boulder. Jake's shoulders slumped.

Emily grinned. "So much for illegal campers, Superman."

"I made a mistake, all right?"

"There's a path, though. Where do you think it goes?"

"The deer must have made it," Jake said.

Emily's eyes lit up. "Or maybe the wolves."

Jake pointed to the bushes behind her. "The path keeps going through there." He might not get to save the island from intruders, but maybe if they found wolf scat or bits of hair, Mr. Timmins would have the proof he was looking for. Or maybe he'd find something even better.

Emily walked over and pulled apart the bushes. "It sort of looks like a path, but I don't think we should go any farther."

"Aw, come on, Em. Maybe we'll find a skull like Mr. Timmins had on his wall." He had to show her he wasn't afraid, even though the idea of two wolves roaming around still made his stomach do backflips.

"I thought you hated those skulls," Emily said.

"I've been thinking about it. If he's a bird-watcher, and has a huge picture of an eagle on the wall, he must love animals. I don't think he really killed them. I think he puts them up there with the shotgun so people will think he's mean and scary." He started down the path. "George told me once that there used to be cows living on the island. That must be how he found the big skulls. Maybe we can find one too. Or maybe we can find evidence to show the wolves were here."

Emily followed. "Since when did you get so brave and smart?"

Jake turned away to hide his smile. "I'm not being brave. I want to find a skull to hang on my bedroom wall. And I've always been smart."

"I don't think Sierra would like the skull."

Jake pushed through the salal leaves, watching the ground and trying to follow the path. "You're right. I wish I didn't have to share a room with her."

"I'd love to have a sister."

"That's what you think. Trust me, you'd get bored of it pretty quick." He pushed a salal branch out of the way. It snapped back into Emily's face.

"Hey!" Emily rubbed her face. "That hurts."

"Sorry." Ahead of him, the sun cut through the branches. "We're in another open space. The path ends here."

He stepped onto the dried grass and waited for Emily to catch up. A large prickly bush grew in the center of the clearing. Emily ran toward it.

"Blackberries," she called.

"I told you we'd find something cool." Jake grabbed three berries and shoved them into his mouth. The warm juice trickled down his throat.

"These are delicious," Emily said.

They spent the next half hour picking and eating berries. Jake wiped the sweat off his forehead. He could feel the sun burning the back of his neck.

"It's roasting. I need some shade." He sat down on a log at the edge of the clearing. Emily dropped beside him on the moss.

"I didn't know blackberries grew on Hidalgo," Jake said.

"This is the first bush I've ever seen. I wonder if anyone else knows about it."

Jake looked into the trees behind him. Huge cedars loomed above a layer of red dirt and small twigs. Deeper in the forest, a green carpet of moss covered everything, even the tree trunks.

"I bet that moss would make a comfy bed," said Jake.

"It would be soft," said Emily, "but probably wet. Moss grows best in damp areas. I bet this clearing is a swamp in the wintertime."

"I can think of worse places to be stranded."

"I'd rather be home in my own bed, or at least have a sleeping bag," Emily said. She stood up and brushed off her pants. "Let's go back to the beach. It must be getting close to lunchtime."

Jake stood and looked around. The trees swayed above him, and a faint breeze blew through the clearing. "How do we get home?"

"We follow the path, of course." She turned in a circle. "Where is it?"

He pointed to the far side of the grass. "That's it over there."

Emily ran to the other side. "No, here it is."

Jake walked to where he had pointed. "No, I'm sure this is it. We followed the path, and when we came out, the blackberries were right in front of us." When he turned his back to the path, he could see the blackberry bush.

Emily did the same from her path. "I see blackberries in front of me too."

Jake pushed aside the salal bushes, trying to see where the path led. "Can you see the boulder?" he called.

Emily peered into the bushes. "No, can you?"

"No." Jake walked back into the clearing.

The first feelings of panic rose up inside of him. He thought back to when he led them along the path, and the bushes he had pushed out of the way.

"I know why too. We had to cross a lot of forest before we got to the blackberries," he called across the grass. "I don't know which way we started from. We shouldn't get too far apart." He rubbed his arms. The air had gotten cooler.

Emily jogged to Jake's side. The forest around them looked the same everywhere—big trees, moss and streaks of sunlight.

"I hate to say this," said Emily, "but I think we're lost."

"We can't be lost," Jake said. "Cook's Point isn't big enough. We're just too far into the bushes to figure out which way to go." Even as he spoke, the panic grew worse. He looked at Emily in horror. She confirmed his worries by biting her lip. "We're not on Cook's Point anymore, are we?" he said.

"Nobody has ever mentioned the blackberries before," Emily replied. "We would have heard about them if they were on the point. You know when we were following the deer?"

"And we went uphill, and you said we weren't going past the hill?"

Emily nodded. "Um, yeah. I think maybe we went past the hill after all."

"So we're lost in the middle of the forest, no one knows where we are and we have nothing to eat or drink?" Jake's voice rose with every word.

Emily scrunched her nose. "Yep."

His body flashed with heat. He wanted to drop to the ground and curl into a ball. How would they ever survive? They were goners.

# Chapter Seven

Jake took a deep breath and tried to calm himself down. Panicking wasn't going to help. "What are we going to do?"

Emily didn't answer. She was staring into the trees, her lips pressed into such a tight thin line that they'd almost disappeared. Jake couldn't believe it. Was she scared?

She gave herself a shake and focused her eyes on Jake. "We've got to find our way back before dark. The wolves might come out in the evening, especially this far from the road."

Jake had forgotten about the wolves while he and Emily were eating blackberries. He closed his eyes and took another deep breath.

"We need to start walking and find our way home," Emily said.

"Nuh-uh," said Jake, happy to know more than Emily for once. "We learned about safety in school this year. If you ever get lost, you should stay where you are. This may be an island, but it would still take us a really long time to walk to the other end if we chose the wrong direction. Besides, it isn't like we'd be walking along the road. There are swamps and bushes and prickles to go through. It could take us days. And we have no water. We're staying here."

"Then what are we going to do?" Emily asked. "You got us lost. Why don't you figure out how to get us out of here?"

Jake jumped up. "I got us lost? What are you talking about? You're the one who wanted to follow the deer."

Emily pointed a finger at his face. "You wanted to see who was camping in a boulder. We could have found our way back from the deer."

"You ate as many blackberries as I did." He grabbed a stick and broke it in two. "You're always telling me I'm a chicken and that I should take more chances. I finally did, and now you're blaming me for getting us lost."

Emily threw her hands up. "I'm sorry I ever called you a chicken." She strode to the other side of the clearing and started shredding salal leaves.

Jake glared at her. How could she blame him? He turned his back to her and kicked at a tree. They had to wait here until someone came to rescue them. And he didn't care if they spent the whole time not talking to each other.

Emily strode back to Jake. He got ready for more yelling. He already had his arguments planned.

"We need to figure out what to do," she said.

Jake kept his back to her. "Do you promise not to ever call me a chicken again?"

Emily sighed. "I won't call you a chicken anymore."

"And do you admit that you were the one who got us lost?"

Emily stamped her foot. "I didn't get us lost!"

Jake smiled. "I'm kidding." Then the fear came back and lodged in his throat. "How long do you think we'll have to wait until somebody comes to look for us?"

"Your mom said to be back by lunchtime."

"Yeah, she'll be mad when I don't show up to look after Sierra."

"She'll probably go talk to my mom and dad, and after a while they'll start looking for us. But they'll start with all the houses and paths on Cook's first. It will be a few hours for sure before they come anywhere near here, if they do at all."

"We'll be starving by then," said Jake.

Emily sat on a log. "Stop exaggerating. We'll be hungry, but not starving. I have a granola bar in my pocket. We'll have to go look for some water if no one comes to get us by tomorrow."

"By tomorrow? I really don't want to spend the night on a moss bed," Jake said.

"You thought it would be okay before," said Emily.

"That's when it wasn't for real!" Jake shouted. "I spent the night on our deck once, with my dad. The mosquitoes came out after dark, and then it got cold, and then the bats flew around." He waved his arms in the air. "We don't have bug spray or sleeping bags or my dad to scare away the bats."

"We'd better do something then, or we'll be out here with the bugs and the bats," Emily said. Her lips disappeared again before she sighed and turned to face him. "What else did you learn in your safety class?"

Jake thought for a moment. "I know. The teacher said to make lots of noise so that anyone looking for us might hear." He began to yell. "Hello, is anybody there? We're over here. Help! Help!" After a few minutes he stopped. "It's no use."

"It's a good idea, but we can't shout all afternoon. How about every few minutes one of us takes a turn?" suggested Emily.

Jake nodded and sat on a log. "Want to play 'I packed my grandmother's trunk' while we wait?"

"Sure."

"I packed my grandmother's trunk, and in it I put an apple," began Jake.

"I packed my grandmother's trunk, and in it I put an apple and a tent," said Emily.

"I put in an apple, a tent and a shotgun," said Jake.

"I thought the shotgun scared you."

"It doesn't matter," replied Jake. "It's a game. Besides, if we had one, we could defend ourselves against the wolves."

Emily rolled her eyes. "In it I put an apple, a tent, a shotgun and a compass."

On they played. Between turns they shouted for help. After a long while, Jake hesitated on his turn.

"I packed my grandmother's trunk, and in it I put an apple, a tent, a shotgun, a compass, a chocolate bar, a jug of water, bubble gum, a book, the outhouse, Sierra, a cedar tree, an ant colony, an...an...an...oh no, what's next?"

"I win!" Emily jumped off the log and danced around. "An ant colony, gummies, a baby and seaweed." She sat down again and looked at Jake. "Oh, stop pouting. At least we wasted more time."

"I think we wasted a lot of time. My stomach's grumbling. Where's that granola bar?"

Emily hesitated. "I think we should wait. What if we have to stay out here all night?"

"Come on, Em. I'm starving. It's already been ages. Look at how far over the sun is now."

"Okay." Emily dug the granola bar out of her pocket. She broke it and passed half to Jake. "You're right about the sun. When we first sat down, it was shining on that side of the trees, and now it's on the other side."

Jake jumped off the log. "That's it!"

"That's what?" asked Emily.

"I know which way to go."

Emily frowned. "You said we should stay in one place."

"I know, but the sun can show us which way to walk. We watch the sunset from our porch every night." He swung his arm in an arc. "The sun's moving that way. If it goes in the same direction, then it will set over there." Jake pointed behind their heads. "If we walk that way we should find the road."

"I can't believe we didn't think of that before," said Emily. She stood and, following the direction of Jake's finger, began looking in the bushes. "That means the path must be over here." After a few minutes of searching, she returned to the clearing.

"I still can't find the trail," she said.

"It doesn't matter, I know which way to go," said Jake.

"How will we know that we're still going in the right direction?" asked Emily.

Jake smiled to himself. Again he had the answers, not Emily. "Easy. The sun is over our left shoulders now. As long as we keep it there, we know that we're going in the right direction. When we get to the road, we can figure out which way to go to get to Cook's Point."

"Are you sure we should leave?" asked Emily. "What if it doesn't work?"

Jake hesitated. If they stayed, they might never be found. If they left, they might get even more lost. What should he do?

He thought for a few seconds. He felt sure he knew how to get home. He nodded at Emily. "Yep, let's go."

They set off through the woods, keeping the sun over their left shoulders. It wasn't as easy going as Jake remembered. To find a clear path through the bushes and logs he had to veer off course, check for the sun and then try to get back in the right direction. It seemed a lot longer than it had on the way to the swamp. What if he made the wrong decision? He fiddled with a pebble inside his pocket. If they walked in the wrong direction on such a big island, they could be in an even worse situation. And the wolves still lurked in the corner of his mind. He had told Mr. Timmins they wouldn't go into the forest, and here they were, past the hill, deep in the woods, and nobody knew where they were.

He swung his legs over a log, stood up and checked for the sun. He and Emily both walked quietly, lost in their own thoughts. He straightened his back and shoved the pebble deeper into his pocket, deciding that since they were already out of sight of their original spot, they might as well keep going.

"Jake," asked Emily, "doesn't it seem like we've been walking for too long? It only took a few minutes to get to the clearing before."

"I know. I think we're going in the right direction, but we're walking on a diagonal now. We should meet up with the road soon."

They continued, jumping over logs and walking around trees. Prickly Oregon grape bushes scratched Jake's ankles, and thick salal leaves rubbed against his arms. Flies and mosquitoes buzzed around his ears. His throat felt dry and scratchy. They didn't show any of this stuff in *Jungle Hunters*. On TV it all looked fun and glamorous.

He checked the position of the sun and gasped. Dark clouds covered half the circle of sky visible through the trees. As he watched, the clouds marched across the blue as though a giant were wiping the sky with a dirty chalkboard brush.

"We need to move it," he said. "That storm is coming."

A moment later, a flash of light illuminated the forest.

"Lightning!" Emily said.

Jake nodded. He counted in his head. One Mississippi, two Mississippi, three Mississippi...*Boom!* The thunder reverberated through the trees.

"That's pretty close," Emily said.

Jake tried to fix the position of the sun in his mind as the clouds gobbled up the last rays of light. He shivered. The forest darkened.

"Let's get out of here." He pushed faster through the salal, hoping he could keep them moving in the right direction.

The trees creaked and swayed. Cold drops of rain began to fall. Minutes ago he'd been sweaty and hot. How could the weather change so quickly?

Behind him, Emily thudded to the ground. "Ow!" She clutched her ankle.

"Not again," he said. "This isn't the time for jokes."

Emily only rocked back and forth. Her cheeks were flushed.

Jake knelt beside her. "You okay?"

She took a shuddering breath. "My...ankle...hurts." She closed her eyes and banged her fist on the ground.

"Can you walk?"

"I don't know. Hold on a sec," she said.

Jake wiped the rain off his face. Another flash of lightning lit the sky. One Mississip...*Crack!* Jake thought the whole forest had exploded. The ground shook, sending vibrations through his feet and up into his teeth. He ducked his head, expecting a jolt of electricity to surge through him. When he looked up, he saw a huge tree on fire.

Most of the branches and half the trunk had disappeared, as though the giant in the air had reached down and grabbed them for a snack. What remained was a charred Y-shaped trunk split down the middle, with flames shooting out the top.

"We have to go," he shouted at Emily.

She tried to stand up. When she put weight on her leg, she collapsed. "I can't do it!"

Jake looked around frantically. The tree crackled, and sparks scattered to the ground.

"I'll be okay here," Emily said. "You go get help." She slid the bandanna from around her ponytail and began tying it around her ankle.

Jake bit his lip. Lightning flashed. One Miss... *Boom*. He flinched, waiting for a tree to fall on him.

Getting out of the forest was a great idea. They must be close to the road. He could run to Emily's house, get her mom and come back to rescue her. It wouldn't take more than twenty minutes. He'd be a hero.

He stood. "I'll be back soon."

"Hurry."

He stepped away into the bushes, marking the spot where she sat. He saw a clearing ahead that might be the road. It beckoned to him. He imagined warm clothes and a cup of hot chocolate in front of the fire.

Thunder boomed. He checked over his shoulder for Emily. She sat huddled in a ball with her soaking T-shirt stuck to her back. It didn't feel very heroic to leave his friend out in the cold. What would Megafly do? He'd be able to lift Emily with one finger and fly them both to safety. What would his dad do?

Jake turned around.

Emily lifted her head at the sound of his footsteps. "What are you doing? You need to get help."

"I can't leave you alone. Climb on my back."

She smiled. "Thanks." She dragged herself to a stump and pulled herself up until she was standing on one foot; then she heaved herself onto Jake's back. He took a last look at the tree. The rain had reduced the flames to a smoldering hiss. At least they didn't have to worry about a forest fire on top of everything else. He lurched forward, staggered sideways and began plodding through the trees.

Rain dripped into his eyes. He couldn't wipe it away, since his hands were interlaced under Emily. Bushes he hadn't noticed before leaped in front of him. Lifting his leg to step over a log took all his strength. The woods had gone from dry and dusty to wet and slimy. He watched every step to make sure he didn't slip.

"Don't squish that slug," Emily said.

Jake almost dropped her and continued on alone. "I'm doing the best I can," he said through clenched teeth.

"Sorry," she said in a small voice. "I didn't know I was so heavy."

"Neither did I. Do you have rocks in your pockets?"

Emily's body stiffened.

"What?" he said. "It was a joke."

"Look over there," Emily whispered. "Is that a wolf?"

# Chapter Eight

Fear rushed through Jake's body like lightning exploding a tree. He inched his head around and looked where Emily was pointing. A wolf stood as still as the boulders on the beach, but Jake knew this was the real thing. Two icy blue eyes studied him from between the soggy hemlock branches twenty paces away. He saw a wet black nose, patches of white and gray fur, and a body bigger than a large dog's.

Jake waited for Emily to do something, but she just squeezed her arms around his neck.

"Quick, get off and crawl into that salal bush," whispered Jake.

Emily slid off his back, grunting as she landed on her sore foot. She dropped to the ground and pushed her way into the dense bush.

Jake turned to face the wolf. Flames of fear coursed through his body, licking at his legs, shooting all the way up to his head. What had Mr. Timmins said? *Never do anything to make it come closer.* Right. As if he would tempt it toward him with his last crumb of granola bar.

The wolf snaked around the bushes in his direction. Jake's vision grew fuzzy. The wolf's shoulders rocked with each step, like a lonesome cowboy swaggering toward a sheriff, ready for a duel.

Jake wiped the sweat off his forehead. Think! *Throw things at it and back away.* He wasn't very good at estimating, but the wolf could reach him in a few bounding leaps. It had to be a lot closer than one hundred meters.

It didn't look scared. Why was it stalking Jake? Everyone said that wolves hardly ever acted aggressive toward people. What had he and Emily done to anger it? *NEVER run.* Jake's feet twitched. They wanted to sprint. But he couldn't leave Emily.

That left only one thing to do. Jake took a deep breath and stood up tall. He snarled and waved his arms above his head.

"G-g-get! Get out of here, wolf! Shoo! I-I mean it!" he stammered.

The wolf stopped and looked at him. Jake stared back into its blue eyes. He imagined it sizing him up, wondering if he was worth a fight. He heard Emily breathing. Would the wolf believe Jake was more powerful? Would it come closer? Would it attack them? Jake curled his fingers into a fist.

He stamped his feet on the ground and waved his arms in the air. The wolf didn't come any closer. Jake felt stronger.

He saw a log out of the corner of his eye. Without breaking eye contact with the wolf, he climbed on it. He would look scarier if he stood taller.

"Get lost! Grrrrr!" Jake shouted and growled at the wolf, baring his teeth and throwing his arms forward. The wolf took a small step back. Jake glared at it.

"Go on! Leave!" Jake didn't feel so scared anymore. The fire in his body gave him power. He *was* stronger than the wolf. He *would* chase him away.

Jake noticed how skinny the wolf was. And that its scraggly fur hung in clumps. He started to feel a little sorry for it—pushed out of its home by the other wolves. It probably thought it had found territory for itself, and now he was telling it to get lost.

"Jake," Emily whispered, "don't stop."

The wolf had inched toward him. He had to show it who was boss.

"Oh no," Emily said. "Look behind you."

Jake spun around. Another wolf had crept up behind them and was eyeing them from ten paces away. This wolf was a little smaller, with darker fur.

"They hunt in packs." Emily's voice sounded high and squeaky.

Jake swiveled his head from one wolf to the other. He could only concentrate on one wolf at a time. He faced the first wolf again. It had edged even closer while he had been distracted by the other one.

"Go!" Jake shouted at it. The wolf bared his teeth.

With the dark-haired wolf ready to lunge at his back, Jake didn't feel fierce anymore. He would never chase either wolf away as long as he kept thinking about the dark wolf lingering behind him.

In his mind, Jake scooped up the dark wolf and rolled it in a net. The only way to focus on the first wolf was to pretend it was the only one around.

"Scram!" Jake shouted. He imagined an eagle chasing intruders from its nest.

The wolf inched backward.

Keeping eye contact, he picked up a rock and threw it. It landed beside the wolf's front paws. The wolf took another step back.

"Get out of here!" Jake shouted. The wolf lowered its head to its paws, then turned and loped into the woods.

Jake whirled to face the other wolf, arms raised. "You too. Get out of here!"

The dark-haired wolf was already trotting into the forest.

"That's right," Jake yelled. "And don't come back!" As the wolf disappeared into the trees, Jake sank to the ground and took a deep breath. It felt like the first time he had breathed since the wolves appeared.

Emily pulled herself out of the salal. Pine needles and dirt covered her from head to toe. She hugged him.

Jake blushed and wriggled out of her grasp. "I can't believe I chased them away." Now that the wolves had left, Jake's knees felt weak. His hands began to shake. Inside, a warm glow replaced the fire, and bubbles of happiness filled his chest. "Let's get out of here before they come back. I don't want to do that again."

Emily climbed onto his back. He had so much energy after standing up to the wolves that she didn't feel heavy at all for the first few steps. He strode over stumps and through salal bushes. Water dripped into his eyes. Wet leaves slapped against his face and arms. His legs burned with the effort of carrying her. He didn't care. All he could think about was getting to the road, getting home, where it was warm, dry and safe from falling trees and hungry wolves.

Jake stumbled as the forest floor fell away in front of him. He caught himself just in time. He was standing on dirt. "We made it!" he shouted. "We're at the road!"

He put Emily down on the ground.

"What are you doing?"

"I need a rest," he said.

He plonked onto the moss. He didn't care anymore how wet or cold he was. All he could think about was resting his aching back and legs.

Emily patted her back pocket. She pulled out a bag. "Want a gummy bear?"

"You've had those in your pocket the whole time?"

"I forgot about them until now. Sierra gave them to me at the end of the walk to George's. There are only a couple left, but maybe they'll give you some extra energy."

"I guess Sierra's not such a pain after all," Jake said. The gummies were warm and sticky, but the sweetness helped soothe his dry throat. He held the bag out to Emily. "Do you want one?"

Emily shook her head. "You need the energy. It's hard work being a hero."

Jake squinted at her through the rain, trying to decide if she was kidding or not. She looked serious. He twisted the bag in his hands and tried not to smile. He hadn't been able to protect Sierra, but at least he'd done something useful while his dad was away.

The wind howled through the trees, followed by another boom that echoed through the forest. A huge branch fell from high in a tree, ripping through limbs and needles before slamming onto the road a few paces in front of them.

Jake gulped. "Let's get out of here."

"Good idea."

Emily climbed onto his back, and he took another plodding step toward Cook's Point. They rounded a corner, and Jake saw the hill dropping away before them.

"We're almost there," he said. Then he heard voices.

"Jaa-key, Emmmily!"

"Jake, Emily!"

"Sierra! Mom! We're here! We're okay!" In a few moments his mom appeared, pushing his sister in a stroller.

"Jakey!" Sierra struggled to undo the stroller buckles. Her cheeks were red and wet, as if she had been crying.

Emily slid off Jake's back and sat on the ground.

"We've been looking everywhere for you," said his mom as she pulled Jake up and hugged him. "I'm so glad you're okay." She released Jake and pulled Emily into her arms. "Let's get out of here, before more trees come down."

Emily got back onto Jake. He staggered forward a few steps.

"What happened?" his mom asked.

“It’s a long story,” Jake said. “Emily hurt her ankle. She can’t walk.”

“You can’t carry her all the way home,” his mom said. “I’ll do it.”

Jake shook his head. “You know your back always hurts, even when you carry Sierra.” He stepped forward on shaky knees. Then he had an idea.

“Hey, Sierra,” he said. “You’re a big girl, right?”

Sierra nodded and smiled.

“Do want to hold my hand and run down the hill?”

His sister grabbed the buckle again and tried to get out of the stroller. Jake knelt down to help her. “Can Emily borrow your stroller?”

Sierra laughed. “Emily’s too big!”

Jake shook his head. “I think she’ll fit. Her foot hurts, and she can’t walk.”

“Like a baby?” Sierra asked.

Emily nodded. “Yup.”

Sierra giggled and jumped out of the stroller. Jake helped Emily hop into the stroller while his mom held it steady. She squeezed into it, draping her legs over the side.

“Smart idea,” his mom said as she grabbed the stroller handle.

Jake smiled. "Thanks."

Sierra grabbed his hand. "Carry me."

He laughed and shook his head. "Uh-uh. I've done enough carrying today. Come on, let's race them down the hill."

Another loud crack came from the trees. Sierra jumped and grabbed Jake's knee. "What was that?"

Jake knelt down and gave her a hug. "It's the wind breaking the trees, but we'll be okay. I'm here to protect you." He stood up and took her hand. "Let's go!"

# Chapter Nine

The next day, Jake woke late in the morning to the steady sound of raindrops on the roof. Sierra's bed was empty. He climbed down the ladder from his bunk and crossed the slippery deck to the main cabin.

As he opened the door, his jaw dropped. His dad was sitting on the couch.

"Good morning, sleepyhead."

Jake ran across the room with a big grin on his face. "What are you doing here?"

His dad pulled Jake onto his lap. Jake was way too big for lap-sitting, but it still felt good.

"Mom called when you were lost. Even though you made it home safely, I decided this was where I wanted to be."

"What about your business conference?"

His dad ruffled Jake's hair. "It was almost over, and I made the contacts I needed to make."

Jake leaned against his dad's chest. "I'm glad you're here."

"Me too."

"Where are Mom and Sierra?" Jake asked.

"Mom took her to puddle jump. She said you should tell me your story without Sierra around."

Jake nodded. Sierra didn't need to know that the Big Bad Wolf really had tried to eat him. He wriggled onto the couch beside his dad and recounted the previous day's events. His dad leaned forward and grabbed Jake's leg when he reached the part about the wolf. He gripped tighter and tighter.

"That kind of hurts," Jake said.

"Oh, sorry." His dad released Jake's leg. "How did you get away from the wolf?"

Jake continued his story, finishing with finding his mom and Sierra. His dad leaned back and let out a deep breath.

"That's quite a story."

"Yeah. I guess we were pretty lucky to get out of there safely."

His dad sat in silence for a moment. "It was more than luck. You made some courageous choices out there. I'm proud of you."

Jake squirmed. "Thanks." He watched the rain fall on the soggy ground. What if they'd spent the night outside? He didn't even want to think about it. "Do you know how Emily is?"

"I haven't heard. Why don't you walk over and find out?"

When he reached Emily's house, Jake was surprised to see Mr. Timmins sitting beside her in the living room. Her ankle was wrapped in a stretchy pink bandage and propped on the coffee table.

She waved at Jake. "I went to see Dr. Campbell last night. He said my ankle's probably sprained, but I need to go to the mainland for X-rays and to get crutches." She grinned. "Until then you'll have to push me in the wheelbarrow."

He laughed. "It'll be easier than carrying you on my back." He turned to Mr. Timmins. "Did you hear about the wolves?"

Mr. Timmins nodded. "The whole island is talking about it. I told you not to go looking for them."

"Yeah," Jake said.

Mr. Timmins tapped him on the knee. "I hear you were a hero."

Jake blushed. "Not really. What's going to happen to the wolves?"

The old man narrowed his eyes. "Earlier this morning people were talking about shooting them."

Emily gasped.

"I called the conservation officer in charge of this area to put a stop to that. They used to trap them and relocate them, but they don't do that anymore. Someone is coming tomorrow to try to scare them off the island."

"How will they do that?" Jake asked.

"They'll use bear bangers to scare them away from the populated areas. With any luck, they'll decide the island isn't safe and swim away. I imagine all the parents will keep a close watch on their kids until that happens, which suits me just fine."

Jake raised his eyebrows at Emily. It sounded like Mr. Timmins didn't want them to visit anymore.

Mr. Timmins heaved himself out of the chair. As if he'd been reading Jake's mind, he said, "You two are different. Come by whenever you like. Except at naptime."

"We will," Emily called, "as soon as I get crutches."

That night Jake lay in bed working on his comic strip. His mom had given him a battery-powered light that stuck to the wall and shone on his pictures. He had started on a comic strip with a new hero. Eagle Boy rescued small children and animals using his powerful eyes. In the episode Jake was drawing, Eagle Boy stood between two small boys and a mother bear. He used his laser vision to stare down the bear and chase her away.

Jake smiled as he colored in the final frame. He tucked his pencil inside his notebook and slid it into the crack between his mattress and the bunk frame. Before turning out the light, he listened to the noises of the night. Waves crashed on the beach, a mosquito buzzed somewhere in the bunkhouse and Sierra breathed deeply. No wolves howled. He hoped they would be happy wherever they wound up.

The bunkhouse darkened as Jake turned out the light. He pulled the covers around his chin and snuggled under the blankets. The wolves were gone, but who knew what adventure tomorrow would bring? It didn't matter. Eagle Boy was ready for anything.

Acknowledgments

Many people have helped me on my writing journey. I have learned so much from the Vicious Circle, aka the Whistler Writers Group. I treasure our critique-group meetings and your insightful comments. Thank you, Stella Harvey and the VC board, for your tireless work in creating a writing community in Whistler.

Paulette Bourgeois, the Vicious Circle's writer-in-residence extraordinaire, helped me take this book to the next level. Rebecca Wood-Barrett saw me through the fog of the hero's journey and gave her time generously to read my manuscript.

Along the way I've benefited from critiques and readings by Caroline Adderson, Mary Schendlinger, the MCG critique group, Nicole Fitzgerald, Emma Cox, Sharon Broatch and Ellen Bartlett. Thanks to you all.

I am grateful to Sarah Harvey, my editor at Orca, for her professionalism and encouragement.

My parents, Norm and Johanne, have supported and encouraged me since I first showed them the manuscript. Thank you for your love, advice and endless readings.

My husband Duane had the idea that sparked the project. Ben and Julia learned to sleep, giving me time to write. My family has surrounded me with love and support. I love you all so much. Thank you.

Sara Leach lives in Whistler, British Columbia, with her husband and two children. She is the teacher-librarian at a local elementary school, where she shares her love of children's literature with her students. When she isn't writing or teaching, she likes to ski, dance and read. Every summer since she turned three, she has spent time on an island in the Strait of Georgia. Although she's never run into a wolf, she's heard them howling in the night.